Jared's
Last Carrot

Jared's Last Carrot

Published by Wisdom House Books, Inc.
Chapel Hill, North Carolina 27514 USA • 1.919.883.4669 • www.wisdomhousebooks.com

Wisdom House Books is committed to excellence
in the publishing industry.

Book design copyright © 2019 by Wisdom House Books, Inc.
All rights reserved.

Cover and Interior design by Krystal Smith
Cover and Interior Illustrations by Talitha Shipman

Published in the United States of America

Hardback ISBN: 978-1-7331490-0-6
LCCN: 2019907663

1. JUV002210 | JUVENILE FICTION / Animals / Rabbits
2. JUV039060 | JUVENILE FICTION / Social Themes / Friendship
3. JUV039140 | JUVENILE FICTION / Social Themes / Self-Esteem & Self-Reliance

First Edition
14 13 12 11 10 / 10 9 8 7 6 5 4 3 2 1

Jared's Last Carrot

Sara Devine

Illustrated by
Talitha Shipman

Wisdom House Books

Jared tossed and turned under the bright morning sun.
He opened his eyes and licked his lips.
"What a yummy dream," he whispered.

He hopped out of bed, stretching all the way from
his big bunny feet to his long bunny ears.

That's when he heard a strange sound . . .
blub, blub, blub, blub . . . .

He looked down and saw his belly move!

Jared raced to the kitchen.

"Yes! Carrot pancakes! Why haven't I thought of this before?" He laughed so loudly that all the mice skittered back into their little hole.

He couldn't stop thinking about his dream. "They will be so delicious! I will add loads of maple syrup, and I'll even have a fluffy, white mountain of whipped cream going all the way to the ceiling! How bunnytastic!"

Jared grabbed Grandma Betty's Recipe Book
and gathered all the ingredients he would need
to make the pancakes:

 Three tablespoons of oil and
one cup of flour.

 An overflowing cup of buttermilk
for a hint of something sour.

 A tablespoon of sugar,
a pinch of pink sea salt.

 And one teaspoon of baking
powder to finish the list off.

Jared had every ingredient,
except for the most important one.

He looked in his fridge, way in the back past his jug
of carrot cream and the jar of pickled carrots,
but he couldn't find a single carrot.

His belly rumbled again.

Grabbing a basket and tools, he went to his garden. Harvest time was over, but still he began to dig in hopes of finding one last carrot.

Hours passed. Morning was nearly over.
The noonday sun beat down on Jared,
and still his basket was empty.

He thought about the carrots he loved so much.
He thought about their crunchy,
orange sweetness and delicious leafy greens.
He imagined all the ways they could be cooked:
boiled and broiled, sautéed and stir-fried.
Stews and pot-pies. Carrot pancakes . . . .

He hoped against the odds.

"Twinkling stars, blessed sky,
Earth so full of surprise . . .
May you hold just one last carrot,
waiting for me to find."

He continued digging. His shovel hit what felt like a rock.
He pulled and pulled until finally it broke free.
It was shiny, yellow, and carrot shaped.
He had never seen anything like it.

It had to be a carrot!

Hauling it to the kitchen, his tummy rumbling,
Jared was ready to make his carrot pancakes at last.

First, he tried to slice it with a knife.
He tried to peel it, tried to dice it,
he even tried to break it with a hammer.
Nothing worked!

He sat for a while with tears in his eyes,
until he had an idea.

"I'll ask my neighbors!
I'm sure one of them can help me."

As soon as the idea popped into his head,
he remembered that he had never given any of
his neighbors a single carrot, or bowl of sugar,
or anything when they needed it.

Jared was sure they would treat
him the way he treated them.

But, when his belly rumbled once more,
he decided he would try anyway.

From house to house he went, and just as he guessed,
everyone said no. They had nothing to spare.

With only one house left, Jared sobbed.
"I'm too tired. I just want to go home."

Turning on his heel, he was heading home when the door to the last house on Sunny Lane opened, and Jared's friend, Buddy, walked out.

Buddy was taking out his trash. He waved at Jared.
"How are ya, pal? What're you up to?"

"Hi Buddy," Jared tried to smile.
"I'm okay. I was asking if anyone had carrots to spare,
but no one does, so I was on my way home."

"What? You didn't think to ask
your good friend, Buddy?"
He put his paw on Jared's shoulder.
"It's the end of the season for everyone!
To keep from wasting any carrots,
I used the last of mine to make carrot pancakes.
I have stacks and stacks of them inside.
Have you eaten yet today?"

Jared was so happy he almost cried.
"I wanted carrot pancakes more than anything in
this world! I dreamed about them all last night!"

"Well, it looks like your dream is finally coming true,"
Buddy giggled. "Come on inside."

Over breakfast, Jared told Buddy about the golden
carrot. He fetched it for Buddy to see.

"It sure is beautiful. It looks like solid gold!"
He knocked on it with his fist. "If it is, you could
have a fortune on your hands!"

"You think so?" Jared asked, perking up.

"Well, it's certainly not your everyday carrot.
If I were you, I would take it right to the market
and see how much I could get for it."

The next day, Jared went to the
market like Buddy suggested.
When shoppers saw his golden carrot,
they wanted to touch it and asked plenty
of questions like, "what is it?"
and "what do you do with it?"
"How did it grow?"
and "do you have any more?"
Many shoppers wanted to know
how much Jared would sell it for.

But there was one shopper who fell
deeply in love with the golden carrot.
Mr. Ted, the millionaire fox, in his dapper
furry suit, wanted the carrot so badly that he
beat all other bids that were made for it,
and made an offer that Jared couldn't refuse.

With the money, Jared bought barrels of seeds and vegetables, enough so that he would never run out. He couldn't wait to share the news, and some carrots, with his best friend, Buddy.

In celebration, he prepared a surprise dinner of carrot casserole for everyone on Sunny Lane.

As they ate, Jared thanked all his neighbors,
especially Buddy, whose big brain had given him
the idea to sell his golden carrot.

With a smile full of love, Jared said to Buddy,
"Most of all, I'm thankful to you, my friend, for your even
bigger heart, which has helped me learn to share."

Sara Devine (Author)

Sara lives in Teaneck, New Jersey, where she enjoys singing and writing her own books and music. She performs all over the world as a backup vocalist for music artists, as well as showcasing her own music. Growing up in a large family with nine siblings, food was always a focal point—and, thankfully, was always available. Now, as a grown-up foodie with her own children, Ella and Olivia, Sara has shared this love by creating characters like Jared who also understand this love of food. She hopes children all over will enjoy Jared's story of food and friendship.

Talitha Shipman (Illustrator)

Talitha Shipman was born and raised in Fort Wayne, Indiana. She has always loved art, and as soon as she could hold a crayon she was hooked. She has illustrated several children's books, including *Everybody Says Shalom* by Leslie Kimmelman (Random House, 2015), *Applesauce Day* by Lisa J. Amstutz (Albert Whitman, 2017), and *First Snow* by Nancy Viau (Albert Whitman, 2018). Talitha lives in her hometown with her husband and daughter.

9 781733 149006